Mermaid Mystery

ROSIE BANKS

Wishing Star Palace

With special thanks to Anne Marie Ryan
For Jenny Wilson – I wish we had magic
necklaces like Mia and Charlotte!

ORCHARD BOOKS

First published in Great Britain in 2018 by The Watts Publishing Group

1 3 5 7 9 10 8 6 4 2

Text copyright © Hothouse Fiction, 2018
Illustrations copyright © Orchard Books, 2018

The moral rights of the author and illustrator have been asserted.

A CIP catalogue record for this book
is available from the British Library.

ISBN 978 1 40835 105 5

Printed and bound in Great Britain by Clays Ltd, St Ives plc

The paper and board used in this book are made from wood from responsible sources.

Orchard Books
An imprint of
Hachette Children's Group
Part of The Watts Publishing Group Limited
Carmelite House
50 Victoria Embankment
London EC4Y 0DZ

An Hachette UK Company
www.hachette.co.uk
www.hachettechildrens.co.uk

Series created by Hothouse Fiction
www.hothousefiction.com

The Secret Princess Promise

"I promise that I will be kind and brave,

Using my magic to help and save,

Granting wishes and doing my best,

To make people smile and bring happiness."

CONTENTS

CHAPTER ONE
Crazy Golf

"Yippee!" cheered Charlotte Williams as her golf ball rolled into the hole. "Hole in one!"

Charlotte and her family were playing crazy golf by the beach. Every game had a fun theme. The next one was a pirate ship!

"Race you to the pirate ship!" cried Charlotte Williams, her brown curls flying out behind her as she ran. Her twin brothers,

Liam and Harvey, charged after her but Charlotte got there first.

"My turn!" said Liam. He hit a bright red golf ball with his club and it rolled down the green carpet towards the pirate ship. It stopped just short of the hole, so Liam gave it another gentle tap and it rolled in.

"I'm next!" cried Harvey. "Watch me get a hole in one!"

WHACK! He hit his blue golf ball hard. It rolled off the green carpet, hit the edge and flew into the air.

PLOP! The golf ball fell into a waterfall with a loud splash.

"Oh no!" cried Harvey, staring into the water in dismay.

"Don't worry," said Charlotte. Leaning over as far as she could, she stuck her golf club into the water and fished out Liam's golf ball. She dried it off on her top and handed it back to her little brother. "Good as new!"

"You're the best, Charlotte," said Liam, giving her a hug.

Charlotte took her turn next. "Hey, everyone," she said, hitting the ball. "What did the ocean say to the pirate?"

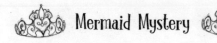

Mum shrugged. "No clue."

"Nothing," said Charlotte, grinning.
"It just waved." She pointed at the Pacific
Ocean sparkling in the California sunshine.
"Get it – *waved*."

Mum and Dad groaned at Charlotte's joke,
but Liam and Harvey laughed.

Mum jotted down their scores then they
moved on to the last hole. It looked like
a fairytale castle. "This reminds me of the
castles back in England," said Mum.

Not long ago, Charlotte and her family
had moved from England to California.

"Mmm hmm," murmured Charlotte. The
crazy-golf castle made her think of her
best friend, Mia Thompson, who lived in

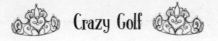

England. But it wasn't because of the castles in England – it was because of a magical palace hidden in the clouds! Even though they now lived far apart, Mia and Charlotte still got to see each other at Wishing Star Palace. They got to go there because they

were training to become Secret Princesses, who used magic to grant wishes!

When it was Charlotte's turn again, she gently tapped the golf ball with her club.

It rolled along the green carpet and dropped
straight into the hole.

"Hole in one!" cheered Dad, giving
Charlotte a high five.

Mum quickly added up the final scores.
"And the winner is … Charlotte!"

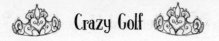

"Charlotte always wins," grumbled Harvey.

"Not always," protested Charlotte. "You win when we play computer games."

"I can't wait until we're as big as Charlotte," said Liam.

Dad chuckled and tousled Liam's curly hair. "Be patient," he said. "I was a little brother too, but now I'm a lot taller than Auntie Liz."

As Charlotte bent down to get her golf ball out, a flash of light caught her eye. The half-heart pendant hanging from her necklace was glowing! Charlotte nearly cried out with excitement – not because she'd won, but because she was going to see Mia!

"I'll go and hand in the golf things," Charlotte offered quickly, collecting her brothers' golf balls and clubs. She returned them at a little wooden hut, but instead of going straight back to her family, she ducked out of sight behind the hut.

Checking that nobody was watching, she held her glowing pendant and whispered, "I wish I could see Mia."

The radiant light from the necklace surrounded her. Charlotte's smile was almost as bright as her pendant because she couldn't wait to see Mia! As the magic swept her away, Charlotte knew her family wouldn't be worried – no time would pass here while she was gone.

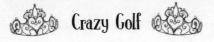

A moment later, Charlotte found herself
standing in the grand entrance hall of
Wishing Star Palace. She was wearing her
pink princess dress and her ruby slippers.

Her brown eyes widened with delight as she spotted a girl in a gold dress sitting on the bottom step of a sweeping marble staircase. There was a sparkling diamond tiara on her long, blonde hair.

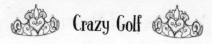

"Mia!" Charlotte called happily.

Mia leapt up and ran towards Charlotte.

As they hugged each other tight, Charlotte's own diamond tiara fell off her head.

"Whoops!" said Charlotte, quickly picking it up.

"Do you suppose we'll get to start the next stage of our training today?" Mia asked Charlotte, helping her put the tiara safely back on her head.

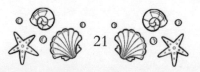

"I really hope so!" replied Charlotte.

Hearing footsteps behind them, the girls turned around. A group of Secret Princesses were coming down the stairs in their swimming costumes!

"Hi, girls!" said Princess Sylvie, whose polka-dotted swimsuit was red like her hair. She was a baker back in the real world, and she had a necklace with a pendant shaped like a cupcake.

"Are you going to the palace swimming pool?" asked Mia.

"Not today," said Princess Evie, who was wearing a floral-print bikini that matched the flower pendant on her necklace. It showed her special talent for gardening.

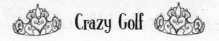

"We're going to the Blue Lagoon."

Mia and Charlotte exchanged excited looks. They'd visited Wishing Star Palace many times, but they'd never been to a lagoon before!

"Oooh! Can we come too?" asked Charlotte.

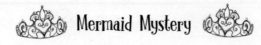

"Of course," said Princess Ella, who had a ruffled leopard-print swimming costume. "That's where you're going to begin the next stage of your training!"

Mia and Charlotte jumped up and down, squealing.

"Yay!" cried Mia. "We can't wait to get started!"

"Then let's use our ruby slippers," Ella suggested, "so we get there fast."

Everyone clicked the heels of their red-jewelled slippers together three times and called out, "The Blue Lagoon!"

WHOOSH!

Magic whisked them high above Wishing Star Palace and across the gorgeous grounds.

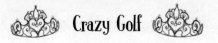
As they flew, Charlotte spotted places she and Mia had visited before – the swimming pool, the roller coaster, and the beautiful butterfly garden. Finally, she spotted a bright aquamarine lake far below.

As she got closer, Charlotte saw a waterfall cascading into the lagoon. Charlotte sat down on one of the rocks around the lagoon's edge and dipped her hand in the water. "It's so lovely!"

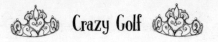

"Look!" cried Mia, pointing across the water. "Someone's already swimming!"

A lady with long, silvery hair waved to them from the water. Suddenly a glittering green fish tail rose up from the surface.

"Oh my gosh!" gasped Charlotte,
clutching Mia's arm.

There was a mermaid in the Blue Lagoon!

CHAPTER TWO
The Blue Lagoon

"You must be Mia and Charlotte," said the silver-haired mermaid, swimming over to them. "My name is Oceane."

She pulled herself out of the water and reclined on one of the rocks. The beautiful emerald-green scales on her wet tail shimmered in the sunlight.

"I didn't know there were mermaids at

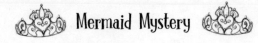

Wishing Star Palace," Charlotte spluttered.

"Oh yes," Oceane said with a tinkling laugh. "Mermaids and Secret Princesses have always worked together."

"The mermaids sometimes help us by making watery wishes come true," explained

Princess Ella.

Oceane blew into a conch shell. A moment later, two more mermaids emerged from the water.

"Come and meet the trainee princesses!" Oceane

called, beckoning them over.

"I'm Coral," said a purple-tailed mermaid
with coppery red hair. She gestured to a
mermaid with bright blue streaks in her black
hair. "And this is Nerida."

Nerida smiled shyly at the girls and waved
her turquoise tail.

"My name's Marina," said the youngest mermaid, who had pale green hair. She winked at Mia and Charlotte, then splashed them playfully with her silvery tail.

"You can play with the girls later," Coral scolded Marina. "First they need to learn about the next stage of their training."

Oceane held the conch shell out to the girls. "Hold it against your ears," she told them. "And listen to your instructions."

Putting their heads together, Mia and Charlotte held the shell against their ears.

For a moment, Charlotte didn't hear anything but the gentle sound of lapping waves. Then a beautiful, otherworldly voice began to sing:

The next jewels to earn are aquamarine.
They sparkle like the sea, all bluey-green.
Help the mermaids grant four watery wishes,
And soon you'll be able to swim like fishes!

When the singing stopped, Charlotte
lowered the conch shell. "So we need to earn
four aquamarines?" she confirmed.

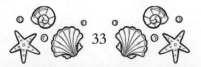

The Secret Princesses and mermaids all nodded.

"What did the bit about swimming like fishes mean?" Mia asked, puzzled.

"Let me show you," said Princess Sylvie. She rummaged around in her swim bag and took out a comb covered in brilliant aquamarines. Sitting down on a rock, she tucked the jewelled comb into her hair.

There was a flash of bluey-green light and Sylvie's legs turned into a tail! She dived into the water, her tail waving at the girls before it disappeared under the surface.

Mia and Charlotte blinked in astonishment. Princess Sylvie had just become a mermaid!

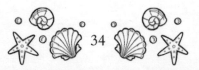

"That's the coolest thing I've ever seen!"
said Charlotte.

"Me too!" Mia gasped in agreement.

Princess Evie showed the girls her own comb. "You'll get your mermaid combs when you've earned four aquamarines," she explained. Sliding the comb into her brown hair, Evie turned into a mermaid, too!

One after another, the Secret Princesses changed their legs into tails and joined the mermaids in the water. Eventually, only Princess Ella remained with Mia and Charlotte.

"That looks so fun," said Mia wistfully.

She and Charlotte took off their ruby slippers and sat down by the edge of the lagoon, sticking their legs in the warm water.

"Come and play!" urged Marina, bobbing up and down in the water.

"We can't," said Mia. "We haven't got swimming costumes."

"I'll give you something even better," said Princess Ella. She waved her wand.

"Oh, wow!" Charlotte gasped, looking down in surprise. Where her legs usually were was a tail with pearly pink scales!

She glanced over at Mia. Her best friend now had a glittering golden tail!

"Oh my gosh!" squealed Mia. "We're mermaids!"

Princess Ella grinned at them. "Go ahead and try out your tails."

Charlotte didn't need any more encouragement! She pushed herself off the rock and dived into the Blue Lagoon.

SPLASH! Mia slid into the water next to Charlotte. "Oooh!" she giggled. "This feels so weird!"

"Let's see how fast these tails can go!" said Charlotte. She plunged underwater and swam to the middle of the lagoon. At first it felt strange not to be kicking her legs, but

it didn't take long to get used to her tail. It moved up and down, propelling her quickly through the crystal-clear water.

Mia swam up to her. Without thinking, Charlotte blurted out, "This is awesome!"

Mia's eyes widened in surprise. "We can talk under water!" she said.

Their mermaid tails didn't just let them swim like fish – they could breathe and talk underwater, too!

Charlotte felt a tap on her shoulder. It was Marina, the youngest mermaid. "You're it!" she said. The mermaid shot off through the water, leaving a trail of bubbles behind her.

Charlotte giggled and chased Marina through the water.

"Gotcha!" she said, tagging her back.

"I'll show you how to do a fin flip," said Marina, turning a somersault in the water. Charlotte, who did gymnastics back in the real world, quickly mastered fin flips – and a few other mermaid tricks too.

Meanwhile, Nerida took Mia on an underwater tour of the Blue Lagoon. It was even more beautiful under the water's surface. Tropical fish darted in and out of coral reefs every colour of the rainbow.

"They're gorgeous," said Mia as a school of hot pink fish swirled around her.

"Those are angelfish," Nerida told her.

"Hello," giggled Mia, as an orange-striped fish swam over and kissed her on the nose.

"That one's a butterfly fish," said Nerida.

When they had finished playing, the mermaids and princesses floated up to the surface, fluttering their tails as they drifted lazily on the water.

"This is so amazing," said Charlotte, making little circles in the water with her hands. "I just wish Princess Alice was here to enjoy it too."

"Why don't you see if she can join us?" suggested Princess Ella.

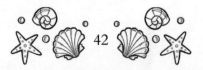

Charlotte spoke into the milky white stone on her magic moonstone bracelet. "Alice?" she said. "It's Charlotte. Can you come to the Blue Lagoon?"

A moment later, Alice magically appeared by the edge of the water.

"Hi, everyone!" she called, waving excitedly. "Sorry that I couldn't come earlier.

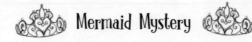

I was in the recording studio."

Princess Alice was a pop star back in the real world, but Mia and Charlotte had known her since before she was famous, when she used to live next door to Mia. She had been their babysitter when they were little and had spotted their potential to become Secret Princesses.

Alice quickly slipped an aquamarine comb into her strawberry-blonde hair, which had trendy red streaks in it. Seconds later she had a long tail covered in pretty red scales.

"So how do you like being mermaids?" she asked, swimming over to Mia and Charlotte.

"It's awesome!" Charlotte said, turning a fin flip and grinning.

"Once you've earned your combs, you can become mermaids whenever you like," said Alice.

Charlotte squealed in delight, but when she looked at Mia, her friend was distracted.

"Earth to Mia," said Charlotte.

"Sorry," said Mia. "I think that frog is watching us."

Charlotte followed Mia's gaze and saw a big, slimy green frog with bulging eyes. It did seem to be staring at them.

"Ugh," Charlotte said.

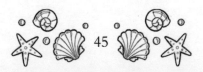

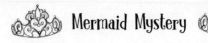

"It's giving me the creeps."

"Aw, it can't help being ugly," said Mia, who loved all animals – even frogs. She called over to Princess Ella, who was a vet back in the real world. "Hey, Ella! What kind of frog is that?"

Princess Ella swam over to the rocks to get a better look.

"Hmm," she said, tilting her head to the side as she studied the frog. "I don't know. I've never seen a frog like that before."

RIBBIT! The frog croaked loudly, then jumped into the lagoon. As it swam around, the Blue Lagoon began to change. A slimy green scum formed on the water's surface.

"Ew!" said Charlotte.

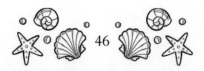

The Blue Lagoon

"What's going on?" cried Merida.

"I don't know!" Oceane shouted back.

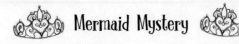

Mia and Charlotte exchanged horrified looks. The frog was turning the Blue Lagoon into a slimy green swamp!

CHAPTER THREE
Freya's Wish

The Secret Princesses quickly swam over
to the side and climbed out of the scummy
green water. They quickly pulled their
magical aquamarine combs out of their hair,
and their tails instantly became legs again.

"This is so gross," said Princess Evie,
pulling a face as she wiped the sticky green
slime off her arms.

The mermaids hauled themselves out of the water and perched on the rocks by the edge of the lagoon. A horrible smell like rotten eggs was wafting up from the water.

"Ugh! It stinks!" said Marina, holding her nose.

"Um," Charlotte called from the horrid green water. "What should we do?"

"Oops!" said Princess Ella. "I forgot you girls don't have combs yet." She helped the girls get out of the water, then fetched her wand and pointed it at them. A moment later, Mia and Charlotte had legs again.

Charlotte wiggled her toes. It felt odd!

"What happened to the water?" asked Coral, looking worried.

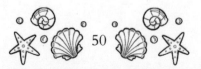

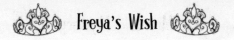

"It was the frog," said Mia. "I'm sure of it."

Charlotte nodded. "The water changed colour as soon as it jumped in."

"But how is that possible?" asked Marina.

The frog swam around the lagoon, cutting through the green slime.

"It's writing a message!" Mia said.

Sure enough, words were appearing on the pond's surface:

My name is Toxin, Princess Poison's new frog.
I changed the lagoon to a stinky green bog.
You banished Princess Poison and she doesn't forgive.
Now the palace's mermaids have no place to live!

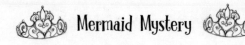

When he had finished writing the message, Toxin hopped out of the water and vanished into thin air.

"We should have guessed that Princess Poison was behind this," said Alice angrily.

Princess Poison had once been a Secret Princess, but she'd been banished from Wishing Star Palace for using her magic to make herself more powerful instead of helping other people. Now she spoiled wishes instead of granting them. Cruel and spiteful, she was always causing problems for the Secret Princesses and the people they were trying to help.

"Where are we going to live?" wailed Marina, her eyes filled with tears.

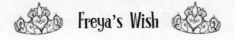
The four mermaids stared at their ruined home in dismay.

"Don't worry," said Princess Ella. "We can use our magic to give you legs."

"But we're mermaids!" sobbed Marina. "We're not supposed to have legs!"

Charlotte understood how she felt. Having a tail had been fun, but she wouldn't want one all the time! "I've got an idea," she said. "Maybe the mermaids can stay in the swimming pool."

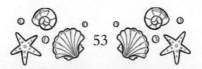

"Good thinking, Charlotte," said Alice. Turning to the mermaids, she said, "You're welcome to live in the pool until we sort out this mess."

"Thank you," murmured the mermaids gratefully.

"I wish we could do something to break Princess Poison's curse," said Mia.

Charlotted nodded. The palace swimming pool was beautiful, but it was much smaller than the Blue Lagoon.

"Perhaps you can," said Oceane. "If you grant four watery wishes and earn your aquamarine combs, the good magic will be strong enough to undo Princess Poison's horrible curse."

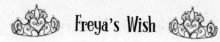

Charlotte didn't need to check with Mia – she knew her best friend would want to help. "When can we start?" she asked eagerly.

"You'll need to check the magic pearl," said Oceane. "To see if a watery wish needs granting."

Mia and Charlotte exchanged confused looks. Normally when a wish was made, the Secret Princesses' wands glowed.

"Before they do that, I think we should send you to the swimming pool," said Princess Alice to the mermaids.

"You're probably right," agreed Coral. "We mermaids mustn't stay out of water for too long."

"You'll be back home soon," Mia promised the mermaids. "We'll break Princess Poison's spell as soon as we can!"

"Please be careful," said Oceane. "Princess Poison is ruthless."

"Mia and I always look out for each other," Charlotte assured her. She and Mia were training to become Friendship Princesses, a very rare type of Secret Princess. They always worked in pairs

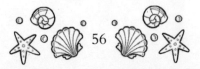

because their friendship
was so strong.

"Thank you," said
Coral. "And good luck!"

Alice waved her wand,
making the mermaids
disappear.

"So where's this magic
pearl?" asked Mia.

"In the cave behind
the waterfall," replied
Princess Evie.

Mia and Charlotte
stepped gingerly over the
slippery rocks, heading
towards the waterfall.

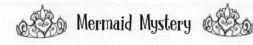

As they got closer, they could see an opening behind it. Ducking under the curtain of tumbling water, the girls entered the cave.

"Cool!" breathed Charlotte, wiping mist off her face and looking around.

An enormous, glowing pearl cast a soft light on the cave's pink coral walls.

Stepping forward, Mia and Charlotte

could see a girl's image shimmering on the pearl's surface. Her skin was tanned and she had curly, sun-streaked brown hair.

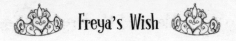

The girls touched the pearl and words appeared:

Freya's made a wish by the water.
Say her name to go and help her!

"Ready?" Charlotte asked Mia.

Mia nodded, then they both called out, "Freya!"

Bubbles rose up and swirled around the girls. As magic carried them away from the cave, Charlotte felt like she was floating through a warm, bubbly bath.

A moment later, the girls arrived on the shore of a lake surrounded by wooded hills.

There was a sandy beach and the shoreline

was dotted with a cluster of quaint wooden cabins. Nearby, a big group of children were playing beach volleyball, but thanks to the magic, nobody had noticed Mia and Charlotte appear out of thin air. Luckily the magic had also changed their clothes to shorts and T-shirts.

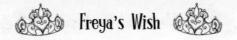

"Can you see Freya?" asked Charlotte.

They watched the volleyball game to see if they could spot the girl from the pearl. A tall boy punched the volleyball over the net. It sailed towards a small girl who was on the other team.

"Get it, Pipsqueak!" yelled one of her teammates.

The small girl jumped for the ball but missed. It plopped on to the sand, right in front of Mia and Charlotte. The other team cheered loudly.

"Way to go, Pipsqueak," an older girl with a long plait said to the small girl. "Thanks to you we lost."

"Of course we did," said a bigger boy,

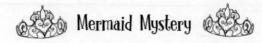

kicking the sand. "Whatever team Pipsqueak's on is bound to lose."

"They're being really mean," Mia whispered.

"I know," said Charlotte. "They shouldn't be bullying that little girl." When the

 girl turned around, she gasped. Pipsqueak was Freya!

"It's her!" Mia whispered to Charlotte.

Freya trudged through

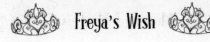
the sand dejectedly to collect the volleyball.

"Hi," said Charlotte, tossing Freya the ball. "This is yours, isn't it?"

"Thanks," said Freya, catching it. "Though I don't know why I bother playing – I stink."

"That was a really tough shot," said Mia sympathetically. "Anyone could have missed it."

Freya shrugged. "That's not how everyone else sees it," she said, tucking the ball under her arm.

"Those kids shouldn't call you names," said Charlotte.

"I'm used to it," said Freya. "I'm the youngest, and I'm small for my age. Every

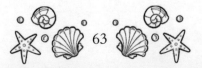

summer it's the same – nobody ever wants me to be on their team."

"That's ridiculous," said Mia indignantly. "I'd be on the same team as you."

Freya smiled at her. "Thanks."

"I'm Charlotte," said Charlotte. "And this is my best friend, Mia."

"Nice to meet you," said Freya. "I'm Freya. So are you two going to join in with the treasure hunt today?"

"What treasure hunt?" asked Mia.

"Every year, my grandad organises a big treasure hunt at the end of the summer holidays," explained Freya. "All the kids staying around here are invited to join in."

"That sounds really fun," said Charlotte.

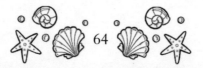

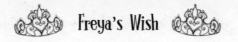

"It is fun," said Freya. She sighed deeply. "But I'm always on the losing team. I really wish I could be on the winning team this year. Then everyone might stop thinking that I'm a loser."

Charlotte caught Mia's eye and she gave a little nod.

"We'd love to do the treasure hunt with you," said Mia.

Charlotte's heart pounded with excitement. They had found out what Freya's wish was. Now they just had to grant it – and break Princess Poison's curse!

CHAPTER FOUR
Mermaid Mystery

CLANG! CLANG! The sound of a bell rang out across the beach. Hearing the noise, kids started running towards a cabin with a big wooden porch.

"What's going on?" asked Charlotte.

"The treasure hunt is beginning," said Freya. "Let's go!"

The girls followed Freya up to the cabin.

An older man with a neatly trimmed white beard and twinkling blue eyes stood on the porch ringing a brass ship's bell. He was wearing a blue and white striped top, a captain's hat and deck shoes.

"Hi, Grandad," said Freya, giving him a big hug.

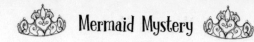

"Looking forward to the treasure hunt, my dear?" Grandad asked, patting her head.

Freya nodded.

Soon the porch was filled with children chatting excitedly.

"These are my new friends, Mia and Charlotte," Freya announced to the group. "They're going to do the treasure hunt, too."

"I wonder what the treasure will be this year?" said the girl with the long plait. "Last year's prize was so cool – a new ping pong table."

"That's my cousin, Ruby," Freya whispered to Mia and Charlotte.

An older girl with a wavy brown bob said, "I really hope I'm on the winning team."

"That's Eden," Freya told Mia and
Charlotte. "She's my big sister."

"Then you'd better hope Pipsqueak isn't on
your team," said a teenaged boy in a baseball
cap, winking at Freya. He had a sunburnt
nose and mischievous green eyes.

Freya stuck her tongue
out at him. "That's
my brother, Josh,"
she told the girls.
"See what I mean
– nobody wants me
on their team. Not
even my own family."

Charlotte smiled at her sympathetically.
Apparently big brothers could be just as

annoying as her little ones sometimes were!

Mia patted Freya's back. "You'll show them," she told Freya encouragingly. "This year you'll prove everyone wrong."

"OK, listen up, kiddos," said Grandad. "This year's treasure hunt is called 'Mermaid Mystery'. A mermaid has hidden a treasure somewhere close to the lake. The first team to find it wins."

Charlotte glanced over at Mia, whose eyes were shining with excitement. Charlotte knew exactly what her best friend was thinking – if they helped Freya to solve the mermaid mystery here, they'd also be helping the real-life mermaids back at Wishing Star Palace!

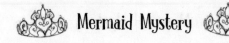

"Josh and Ruby," said Grandad. "You're the oldest so you'll be this year's team captains."

Freya's brother and cousin stood up and started to pick teams. Josh chose his sister, Eden, first, while Ruby picked a tough-looking boy with lots of freckles. The captains took turns choosing until there were only a few kids left.

"Charlotte," called Josh, waving her over. Charlotte went over to join her teammates. She shot Mia a worried look. What if they ended up on different teams? That would be a disaster – they needed to be together to grant wishes!

Charlotte held her breath, waiting to see

who Ruby would choose next. She let out a sigh of relief as Ruby picked a girl with short hair. Then Josh waved Mia over to his team.

"Phew!" Mia said, squeezing Charlotte's hand happily.

Finally, only Freya and a little boy were left waiting to be picked.

"We've got to make sure Freya's on our team, too," whispered Mia. "Otherwise we won't be able to help her."

They went over to Josh. "Can Freya be on our team?" Charlotte asked quietly. "Please?"

Josh looked doubtful. "Pipsqueak never wins," he said.

"It will be different this year," Charlotte promised him.

"Besides, she's our friend," said Mia shyly.

Josh sighed. "Come on, Pipsqueak," he said, beckoning his little sister over. "Don't let me down."

Freya smiled gratefully at Mia and Charlotte. "Thanks," she told them. "I wasn't picked last for a change."

The little boy joined Ruby's team, then Grandad handed Josh and Ruby each an envelope.

"Each team has a different set of clues, but they both lead to the treasure," said Grandad. "Good luck – and may the best team win!"

"That will be us then," said Ruby confidently, striding off with her team.

74

Josh tore open his envelope. He took out a piece of paper and read the words written on it aloud. "The eyes on my front can see, but the eyes on my back are blind."

"That doesn't make any sense," said Josh, frowning.

"It's a riddle," said Mia.

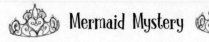

Everyone searched their brains, trying to work out the solution.

"Maybe it's a needle?" guessed Charlotte. "Isn't the hole you put thread through called an eye?"

A curly-haired boy shook his head. "But that sort of eye can't see."

"Maybe the next clue's hidden behind a picture with lots of eyes?" suggested one of Freya's cousins.

"I've got it!" Mia exclaimed. "It's a peacock! They have two eyes on their heads, but their tail feathers look like they've got eyes on them!"

"Of course!" said Josh.

"Way to go, Mia!" said Charlotte, feeling

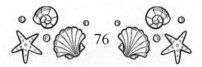

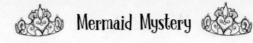

proud of her friend.

Josh frowned. "I still don't get it. There are tons of ducks and geese out on the lake, but I've never seen any peacocks around here."

The children fell silent again, thinking.

"I know!" Freya cried out. "The next clue must be hidden up at Peacock Rock!"

"Pipsqueak, you're a genius!" said Josh, ruffling his little sister's hair affectionately.

Freya's cheeks flushed pink with pride.

"Come on," Josh said, rallying his team. "Let's go and see if Freya's right."

They ran behind the little cluster of cottages into the woods. It was cooler in the woods. Pine cones and twigs crunched underfoot as they followed the path.

"Oh look!" cried Mia as a little animal with brown-striped fur darted out of the undergrowth. "A chipmunk!"

"They're cute, aren't they?" said Charlotte. She had seen lots of chipmunks in California, but she knew Mia was excited because chipmunks didn't live in England.

When they reached the top of the hill they came to a clearing with an enormous blue-grey boulder.

"Oh," said Charlotte, surprised. "I thought the rock was going to be shaped like a peacock."

"Nope," said Freya. "My grandad told me it's called Peacock Rock because the stone is blue, just like peacock feathers. It contains

some mineral that makes it that colour."

The whole team climbed on top of the big rock and looked down over at the lake below. A hawk flew in the cloudless sky, its powerful wings gliding on the gentle breeze.

"Wow!" said Charlotte, breathing in the pine-scented air. "It's so beautiful here."

"What's going on down there?" Mia asked, pointing at the shore.

Small figures on the beach were jumping around excitedly. Their shouts and cheers echoed across the lake.

"Uh-oh," said Eden, jumping down from the rock. "It's the other team. They've found a clue."

"We don't have any time to lose," said Josh. "Let's split up and search. Just be careful – there's a lot of poison ivy up here."

"What's poison ivy?" Mia asked.

Freya pointed to a plant with pointy leaves. "If you touch it, you get a horrible, itchy rash."

Some of the team searched for the clue in

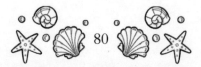

the long grass at the base of the rock, while others hunted in nearby blackberry bushes. Mia, Charlotte and Freya wandered over to a hollow log not far from the boulder. Getting down on her knees, Freya peered inside.

"There's something in there!" she said excitedly.

A flash of blue caught Charlotte's eye. At first she thought it was Peacock Rock, but then she realised it was coming from a much smaller stone – the sapphire on her ring!

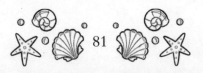

"Mia!" she gasped. "My ring is flashing."

"So is mine!" said Mia, looking down at her hand with a worried look on her face. The girls' magic sapphire rings flashed to warn them when danger was near.

RIBBIT!

A big green frog hopped out of the log.

"Freya!" cried Mia. "Be careful!"

"Don't worry," said Freya, laughing. "It's only a frog. They're harmless."

"Not this one," said Mia.

This was no ordinary frog. It was Toxin – Princess Poison's pet!

"Don't touch it, Freya," said Charlotte. "It's poisonous!"

"But the clue's inside the log," said Freya

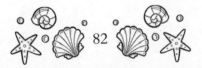

desperately. "I've got to get it."

Toxin jumped towards Freya.

HOP! HOP! HOP!

Freya stepped back in alarm as Toxin sprang closer and closer to her. He was forcing her backwards, towards some bushes.

Mermaid Mystery

"Oh no!" gasped Mia, noticing the pointy leaves on the bushes. Freya was heading straight for a big patch of poison ivy!

"Don't take another step!" called Charlotte.

Freya froze and glanced nervously over her shoulder. She was trapped between a poisonous frog and a big patch of poison ivy!

"We need to help her before she gets hurt!" said Mia.

Charlotte nodded and reached for her necklace. It was time to make a wish!

84

CHAPTER FIVE
Code Breakers

Mia and Charlotte held their glowing
pendants together, the two halves forming a
perfect gold heart.

"I wish to turn the poison ivy into pretty
flowers!" said Mia.

There was a flash of light and the poison
ivy bush turned into a mountain shrub,
covered with gorgeous, pale pink flowers.

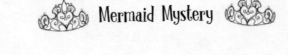
Freya blinked in astonishment. "Whoa. I think my eyes are playing tricks on me."

Shaking her head, she stepped towards the hollow log, but Toxin hopped over – blocking the entrance.

The frog stared at Freya boldly, his eyes bulging and his chest puffed out, as if daring her to take another step.

"Say, Charlotte," said Mia, pointing up at the hawk that was still soaring in the sky. "Do you know what hawks like to eat?"

"Er, no," said Charlotte. She normally loved hearing Mia's interesting animal facts, but she wasn't sure that now was the best time for one!

"Frogs," said Mia loudly. "There's nothing

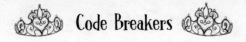

a hawk loves more than a plump, juicy FROG."

RIBBIT!

Toxin shot a nervous look up at the sky and hopped away as quickly as his long legs could carry him.

"Nice work, Mia," said Charlotte, grinning as Toxin vanished in the undergrowth. "You had me fooled – I totally believed you when you said that hawks eat frogs."

"Oh, they do eat frogs," said Mia. "Though I'm not sure a poison one like Toxin would taste very nice!"

"Er, can someone please explain to me what's going on?" said Freya, looking from Mia to Charlotte.

"We'll tell you later," said Charlotte. "Get the clue first!"

Freya reached into the log and pulled out a piece of paper.

"I've got the clue!" she called.

The rest of the team came running over.

"Nice work, Pipsqueak," said Josh, patting his little sister's shoulder. "What does it say?"

"I don't know," Freya said, looking at it with a frown.

They all stared at the piece of paper. Charlotte could read the word "BOAT", but underneath it was an odd jumble of letters – WGLTQURF.

"That's not a proper word," said Eden, trying to pronounce it.

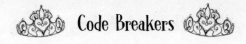

"Does anyone know what this means?" asked Josh, scratching his head.

"Maybe it's a secret code," said Freya.

"How can we solve it?" wondered Mia. "Don't you need a key in order to crack a code?"

They checked inside the log again, to see if they'd missed anything, but there was nothing but moss and dried leaves inside.

Suddenly, Charlotte remembered something that she'd seen in an old film about spies.

"Wait a minute," she said. "I think the word 'boat' might be the key." She grabbed a stick and started scratching letters in the dirt. First she wrote out the normal alphabet.

Then, underneath it, she scratched out a different alphabet, starting with the letters B-O-A-T.

When she was done, the letters on the ground read:

ABCDEFGHIJKLMNOPQRSTUVWXYZ

BOATCDEFGHIJKLMNPQRSUVWXYZ

"It's called a keyword cipher," explained Charlotte.

"I don't understand," said Mia. "How does it work?"

"The cipher alphabet starts with the letters from the keyword, then misses them out later on," Charlotte explained.

"Oh, I think I get it," said Mia, nodding her head. She looked at the clue. The first

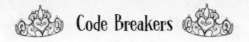

letter of the clue was the same – a W. The second letter was a G. She matched the G on the bottom alphabet with the letter directly

above it. "So the G is really an I."

"Exactly!" said Charlotte.

Using the two alphabets, they matched up every letter in the clue.

"WINDRUSH!" announced Josh when they had decoded the last letter.

"But what's a windrush?" asked Charlotte, frowning. "Is it a type of plant?"

"I bet it's a boat," said Freya, pointing to the keyword.

"I think you might be right, Pipsqueak," said Josh. "That next clue is probably hidden on a boat called *Windrush*. Let's look for it down by the lake."

Josh's team tramped through the woods, heading back down to the water.

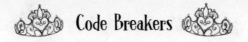

"What happened back there?" Freya asked Mia and Charlotte as they trailed behind the older children. "You did something weird with your necklaces and turned the poison ivy into flowers!"

"It was magic," said Mia.

Freya narrowed her eyes. "Are you teasing me?" she asked them suspiciously.

"I promise we're not teasing," said Charlotte. "Cross my heart."

"It's the truth," Mia said. "Our necklaces let us make three small magic wishes because we're training to become Secret Princesses."

"Whoa!" said Freya, her eyes widening in astonishment. "You expect me to believe you can do magic and you're princesses?"

Mermaid Mystery

"We're not princesses yet," said Charlotte quickly. "But hopefully we will be one day."

"Granting your wish of winning the treasure hunt will take us one step closer," added Mia.

Freya still looked a bit doubtful. "I've never heard of Secret Princesses," she said.

"That's because they're secret," said Charlotte. "So you mustn't tell anyone else on the team what we're doing here."

They walked in silence for a while. "I'm sorry I didn't believe you at first," Freya said eventually. "It's just that Josh and Eden sometimes make stuff up to tease me. And it's so amazing!"

"That's OK," said Charlotte, smiling.

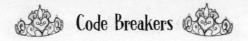

"Sometimes I tease my little brothers too."

When they reached the lake, Charlotte gulped. There were so many boats! Some were floating on the water, others were tied to a wooden dock. Which one was *Windrush*?

"Let's check in the boathouse first," suggested Josh.

They went into a wooden boathouse near the dock. Inside there were wooden racks with canoes, kayaks and dinghies stacked up to the ceiling. The children split up, each checking a different row.

"Has anyone found *Windrush* yet?" Josh called out.

But before anyone could reply, there was a loud *BANG!* The boathouse door had slammed shut.

Charlotte whirled round. She groaned when she saw a familiar smirking face peeking through the small glass window at the top of the door. It was Princess Poison's

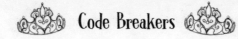
horrible assistant, Hex.

Charlotte went over and
tried to open the door.
It wouldn't budge – Hex
had bolted the door shut,
trapping the team inside.

"Let us out!" Charlotte
demanded.

"That's not a very nice
way to ask," said Hex. Then,
laughing nastily, he sauntered away from the
boathouse.

"We've got to get out of here," said Josh,
throwing his shoulder against the door to try
and force it open. It was no use – the door
stayed shut.

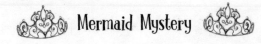

"Help!" everyone shouted, but their cries were drowned out by the sound of cheering in the distance. The other team had found another clue!

"Ruby's team is bound to find the treasure first now," Eden said gloomily.

Charlotte suddenly noticed a small window at the back of the boathouse. Going over to it, she stood on her tiptoes and pushed it open. "Hey, guys," she called. "There might be a way out."

"That's way too small," said Josh. "I can't fit through there."

"Me neither," said Eden.

"I can," said Freya. "But only if you promise not to call me Pipsqueak any more."

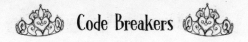

"We promise," said Josh. Eden nodded.

Mia and Charlotte boosted Freya up on to one of the boat racks. Then Freya swung her legs out of the window and wriggled her body through the gap. It was a very tight squeeze!

"I'm stuck!" said Freya.

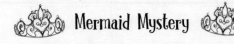

Mia and Charlotte gave her a push and Freya dropped out of sight.

Charlotte heard a loud *OOF!* followed by the sound of footsteps running around the boathouse. The bolt slid in the lock – *CLUNK!* – and the door swung open. They were free!

"Come on, guys," called Freya. "We still need to find the next clue!"

CHAPTER SIX
Digging for Treasure

"Thanks, Pips— I mean, Freya," said Josh as they ran out of the boathouse.

"Yeah," said Eden. "That was awesome."

"I guess being small sometimes comes in handy," Freya told her older siblings, grinning.

The team hurried along the dock. Mia, Charlotte and Freya scanned the names of

the boats tied up to one side of the dock.
There was a *Neptune*, a *Wave Rider*, and a
Lake Belle, but no *Windrush*.

"I found it!" shouted a boy from the end
of the dock. He was standing by a small
sailboat with a rainbow-striped sail.

Just then, a jet ski roared across the water.
It swerved in front of the dock, sending up

a huge spray of water. As everyone jumped
back to avoid getting soaked, the jet ski's
driver untied the sailboat's mooring and
pushed *Windrush* out into the lake.

"Hey!" shouted Josh. "What are you
doing?" He darted forward to grab the
sailboat's rope, but it had already floated too
far from the dock.

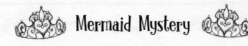

"Oh no," groaned Charlotte, recognising the short, tubby man on the jet ski. "Hex is causing trouble again!"

Its colourful sail flapping in the breeze, *Windrush* drifted towards the very middle of the lake.

"We've lost the clue!" cried Eden.

"That was the same guy who locked us inside the boathouse," said Josh angrily. "I bet he's helping the other team."

"I don't think so," muttered Charlotte grimly. She knew exactly who he was working for – it wasn't the other team, it was Princess Poison!

"We'll have to swim out to the boat," said Josh. "Is anyone wearing a bathing suit?"

Everyone shook their head except Freya.

"I'll get the clue!" she said determinedly.
Freya pulled off her T-shirt and shorts,
revealing a star-print swimsuit underneath.

"Are you sure?" asked Josh doubtfully.
"The boat's out pretty deep."

"I can do it!" insisted
Freya, kicking off her
sandals. "I'm a good
swimmer."

Before her older
siblings could object,
Freya jumped into
the water and started
swimming towards
the boat.

"Freya is really brave," Charlotte murmured.

"Yes, she's gr—"

VRRROOM! VRROOM!

The jet ski revved its engine, cutting off Mia's reply. Hex zoomed back across the lake, riding around the sailboat in circles to churn up the water.

Big waves crashed around Freya. Spluttering, she flailed her arms and legs, struggling to keep her head above the swell.

"Oh no," said Charlotte. "Freya's in trouble!"

"We'd better make another wish," said Mia, putting her golden pendant against Charlotte's own half-heart.

"I wish for Hex to stop and for the water to be calm," said Charlotte.

There was a flash of light and the lake's surface instantly became as smooth as glass.

"Look at that guy!" laughed Josh, pointing across the water.

The magic necklace had turned Hex's jet ski into an enormous, bright yellow inflatable duck!

A scowl on his face, Hex paddled his hands furiously to try and steer the duck.

"He thinks he's in the bath," said Eden, giggling.

Freya had nearly reached the sailboat, her arms and legs slicing through the water. When she got to the boat, she hauled herself into the hull. "I've got it!" she cried, waving a piece of paper in the air.

Everyone cheered from the dock.

"Nice work, Freya!" called Josh.

"Yay!" shouted Eden.

Mia and Charlotte grinned at each other. It wasn't just the two of them who had realised how brave Freya was – her brother and sister were impressed, too!

Turning the tiller, Freya sailed *Windrush* back to the dock. She threw the rope to Josh,

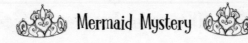

who tied the sailboat back up to the dock. Mia and Charlotte helped Freya out of the boat, then everyone gathered round her to study the clue.

There was a drawing of a berry sandwiched between two sets of letters – on the left were the letters "SA" and on the right it said "ND".

"Ooh!" said Mia. "I love picture puzzles!"

"The next clue must be hidden near some blackberry bushes," said Josh.

"There were lots near Peacock Rock," said Eden. "Let's go!"

Everyone started running down the dock. Suddenly, Charlotte realised that Mia wasn't with them. She turned around and saw that

Mia hadn't moved. She was still staring at the clue.

"What's wrong?" Charlotte asked, running back to Mia.

"I don't think that's right," said Mia. "The clue's not underneath blackberry bushes."

Charlotte put two fingers in her mouth and let out a shrill whistle. The others stopped and turned to see what was the matter. "Come back!" Charlotte called to them.

"What's up?" asked Josh, jogging back.

Mia pointed at the clue. "The berry is in the middle of the word 'SAND'. I think the next clue must be buried in the sand."

"Of course!" said Josh, slapping his head. "That makes sense."

At the end of the dock, they broke into small groups again. They started combing the beach for a clue buried in the sand. Mia, Charlotte and Freya worked together, keeping their eyes on the ground as they talked.

"Did you help me again?" Freya asked the girls quietly. "Did you make the waves go away and change that mean man's jet ski?"

"Yes," admitted Mia. "We used another magic wish."

"Thank you so much," said Freya. "I was really scared. But why didn't anyone else notice what was happening?"

"That's just how the magic works," explained Charlotte.

At the far end of the beach, they found
two pieces of wood arranged in a cross.

"X marks the spot!" cried Freya excitedly.
"I bet this is where the next clue is buried."

"Let's start digging!" said Mia.

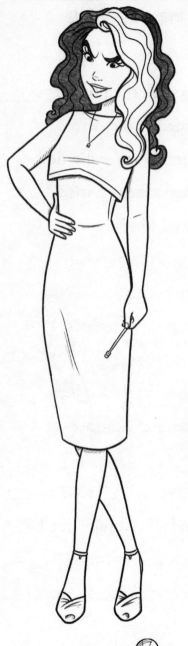

The girls dropped to their knees and started digging with their hands. As they dug through the sand, a shadow fell over them. Charlotte looked up and saw a tall lady in a green dress towering over them. Her hair was jet black except for a streak of white, as icy as her cold heart.

"It looks like you're digging a hole for

yourself," Princess Poison said, her green eyes boring into them.

"Actually," said Charlotte, "we're digging for treasure. So we can grant Freya's wish and earn our aquamarine combs."

"You aren't going to be granting any wishes today," jeered Princess Poison. "Why don't you go home now, because you can kiss your pretty little combs goodbye."

"You're the one who should say goodbye," said Mia defiantly. "You know Charlotte and I never give up."

"Aren't you the feisty one today?" said Princess Poison, laughing mockingly. "But I have a *sinking* feeling that you're wrong."

She took out her wand and pointed it at

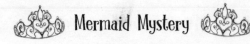

the sand. Then she hissed a spell:

My magic will change this beach in a blink,
I'll turn it to quicksand and watch the girls sink!

There was a flash of green light and Charlotte felt her legs being sucked down. Princess Poison had turned the beach into quicksand. They were sinking fast!

CHAPTER SEVEN
Quick Thinking

Charlotte tried to climb out but the heavy, wet sand was pulling her legs down. She looked around desperately for something to grab on to, but there was nothing around. It was like being trapped in a pot of treacle.

Nearby, Mia and Freya were struggling, too. The sand was sucking them down ... down ... down.

"Help!" cried Freya. "I'm sinking!"

"Well, I'll be going now," said Princess Poison. "You girls are no fun whatsoever – real stick-in-the-muds!" Cackling at her joke, Princess Poison waved her wand and vanished in a flash of green light.

"We need to make a wish," Charlotte said. She held her pendant towards Mia's.

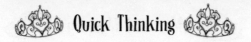
The girls' necklaces were glowing very
faintly now, because they only had enough
magic left to make one more wish.

"I can't reach!" Mia gasped, trying to
get close enough to touch her pendant to
Charlotte's. The wish magic wouldn't work if
their necklaces weren't touching!

"Give me a hand, Freya!" said Charlotte.

Charlotte and Freya each grabbed one
of Mia's arms and yanked with all of their
might.

SQUELCH!

Mia was close enough now to press her
pendant against Charlotte's. "I wish for the
beach to go back to normal," said Mia.

There was a flash of light and suddenly

the quicksand became a fine, powdery beach once more.

"Phew!" panted Charlotte, flopping down on the sand, exhausted.

"We can't take a break!" cried Freya. "We need to find the next clue!"

The girls started digging again, scooping out handfuls of sand.

"I think I've found something!" Freya cried. Rooting around in the sand, she dug out a clear plastic box.

"What's inside?" asked Mia. "Is it the treasure?"

Freya opened the lid, revealing a hand-drawn map inside. "It's not the treasure – it's another clue."

The map showed the lake and the surrounding woods. A treasure chest was marked next to a small bay a short distance from the beach.

"Yoo hoo!" Freya shouted. "We found the next clue!"

The rest of the team came running across the beach towards them.

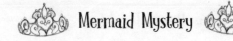

"You're on a roll today," said Josh, winking at his little sister. "We might win after all."

"I know where that is," said Eden, studying the map. "It's Hidden Cove."

"The easiest way to get there is by following the path around the lake shore," Josh said, tracing the route with his finger. "Or we could take a shortcut through the woods."

"I vote for the shortcut," said Eden.

"It won't be easy," Josh warned them. "There's no path."

"But it might be quicker," said Freya. "Let's go!"

"I hope the other team hasn't got there first," said Freya, as they raced towards the

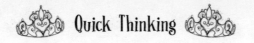

woods. "I can't wait to see the treasure."

"Me too," said Charlotte. She wasn't too bothered about the treasure, but if the other team won, she and Mia wouldn't earn an aquamarine. Glancing back at the lake's clean, clear water, she thought about the lagoon's murky water back at the palace. The mermaids were counting on them to grant Freya's wish!

As they ran past the cabins, a lady with short brown hair waved to them. "How are you getting on?" she called.

"Hi, Mum," said Freya. "I've found lots of clues!"

"Well done, sweetie!" said Freya's mum, giving her a thumbs-up.

"Hey, Mum, have you seen the other team?" Josh called.

"I saw Ruby and some of the others running towards the shore path not long ago," his mother replied.

"Hurry!" yelled Josh. "We've got to beat them to the cove!"

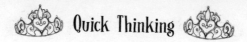

They ran behind the cluster of cabins and dived into a thicket of trees. Josh led the way, forging a path through the dense woods. Birds squawked overhead as the team pushed their way through the branches and brambles.

"Ouch!" said Freya as a thorn scratched her arm.

"Are you OK?" asked Mia.

"I'm fine," said Freya, wiping away a few drops of blood. "I don't want to stop – they'll think I'm a wimp." Scrambling over a tree stump, Freya went on, "Who was that lady who turned the beach into quicksand?"

"Her name is Princess Poison," answered Mia, an anxious look on her face.

"She can do magic like you," said Freya. "Is she a Secret Princess?"

"Definitely not!" said Charlotte. "Princess Poison spoils wishes instead of granting them."

"She used to be a Secret Princess," added Mia. "But she got kicked out."

"I did NOT get kicked out," said Princess Poison, appearing out of thin air. She and Hex were dressed like hikers. They wore green khaki shorts and held hiking poles in their hands. "I CHOSE to leave. Isn't that right, Hex?"

Hex nodded obediently. "Yes, mistress."

"Oh, really?" said Charlotte, raising her eyebrow. "Why would anyone want to stop

being a Secret Princess? It's the best job in the world."

"And who would want to leave Wishing Star Palace?" said Mia. "It's amazing."

"I hear the water there is rather dirty," said Princess Poison, smirking.

"Not for much longer," said Mia fiercely.

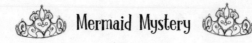

"We're going to break the curse."

"Well then," said Princess Poison, her eyes flashing dangerously. "I'd better start thinking up some new ones."

"Go right ahead. We'll stop you every time," Charlotte said angrily.

"Hurry, everyone!" Josh called from up ahead. "We're nearly there!"

"Come on, guys," said Freya. "She's just trying to slow us down."

As Freya stepped forward, Hex quickly stuck out his hiking pole to trip her. Stumbling, Freya fell to the ground.

"Ow!" she cried, clutching her ankle.

"Oh dear," said Princess Poison. "Your little friend is hurt. Why don't you use a wish

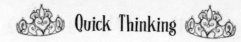

to help her?" She grinned maliciously at Mia and Charlotte. "Oops, I forgot – you don't have any magic left!"

Sniggering, Princess Poison and Hex marched off through the woods.

The others had heard Freya's cry and came back to see what was wrong. "Are you OK?" Josh asked, crouching down by his sister.

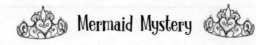

"I twisted my ankle," said Freya, her face pale. From the way her bottom lip was quivering, Charlotte could tell she was fighting back tears.

"Can you walk on it?" asked Eden.

Freya took a few hobbling steps. But every time she put weight on her ankle, she winced in pain.

"I'm too slow," said Freya, a tear finally escaping and rolling down her cheek. "The rest of you go ahead."

"No way," said Josh, shaking his head. "We're a team. We're going to stick together."

Eden nodded. "We need you."

"But you'll lose," said Freya.

"No we won't," said Charlotte.

She and Mia stood on either side of Freya, letting her put an arm around each of their shoulders. Using the two girls for support, Freya was able to hop along. They were slow, but they were moving!

"This is kind of like the three-legged race on sports day," said Mia.

"Only it's a five-legged race," said Charlotte.

Before long, the trees thinned out and they reached the edge of the woods. Standing at the top of a slope, they looked down at a beautiful bay sparkling in the sunshine.

"There's Hidden Cove," said Josh.

"And there are the others!" said Freya, pointing in the distance. Ruby's team were just around the bend, making their way along the path to the cove.

"Run for it!" shouted Josh.

CHAPTER EIGHT
Mermaid Magic

They all hurried towards Hidden Cove.
Charlotte's muscles ached from supporting
Freya, who was hopping along as fast as
she could.

"Not much further," Mia puffed.

They raced down to the water's edge and
came to a halt on a little stretch of sand.

"We made it," gasped Mia.

"Yay!" cried Freya. "We got here first!"

"But where's the treasure?" panted
Charlotte, looking around the peaceful cove.
Aside from a shiny new motorboat tied up
to a dock, there didn't seem to be anything
else there.

"Ahoy!" cried Grandad, emerging from
the boat's cabin. He waved to them from the
polished wooden deck. "Congratulations!
Your team solved the Mermaid Mystery!"

"But where's the treasure, Grandad?" asked
Freya.

"I'm on it," said Grandad, winking. "The
boat is this year's prize. I bought it for all of
my grandchildren and their friends to enjoy."

"Woo hoo!" the children cheered, jumping

up and down on the sand.

Just then, Ruby's team came running around the bend.

"Oh, man," Ruby groaned.

Freya grinned at her cousin triumphantly. "We won," she announced.

"I can't believe you had Pipsqueak on your team and you won," Ruby grumbled.

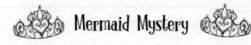

"Actually," said Josh, "we couldn't have done it without her."

Freya beamed with pride.

"Cheer up," Grandad told Ruby. "The winning team get the first boat ride, but I'll take your team for a spin after."

Mia and Charlotte helped Freya into the boat. When the whole team had climbed aboard, Grandad started the engine and steered the boat towards the middle of the beautiful lake.

Mia and Charlotte stood on either side of Freya, holding on to the railing. The breeze whipped their hair as the boat sped across the water.

"Look!" cried Mia, pointing out a fish

leaping in the air. Its silver scales glittered in the sunlight.

"Faster!" cried Freya, clapping her hands.

Grandad pulled on a lever and the boat picked up speed, bouncing over the water.

"This is epic!" cried Charlotte, spray from

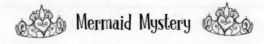

the waves misting her cheeks.

When they reached the middle of the lake, Grandad cut the engine and the boat drifted lazily on the water. The rest of the team went inside the cabin, to explore below deck – but Freya wanted to rest her ankle.

"How does your ankle feel?" asked Mia. She and Charlotte went over to sit next to Freya.

"It's not so sore now," said Freya, gingerly bending her foot up and down. "Thank you so much for your help. Because of your magic I was on the winning team for a change."

"It wasn't just the magic," Mia said. "You were really brave."

Freya smiled at them. "Well, thanks,

anyway," she said. "For making my wish of winning the treasure hunt come true."

SPLASH!

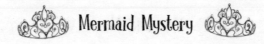

The girls peered over the railing and
caught sight of four sparkly tails waving from
the water. The tails twirled around before
disappearing under the water. Suddenly. four
heads popped out of the water at exactly
the same time. Oceane, Coral, Nerida and
Marina spun gracefully in the water, their
hands over their heads. Then they floated on
to their backs, their fluttering tails forming
a glittering starburst on the water. The
mermaids from Wishing Star Palace were
performing a beautiful water ballet!

"Oh my gosh!" said Freya, her eyes
nearly popping out of her head. "Real live
mermaids! I can't believe it."

Mia and Charlotte grinned. They knew

that the mermaids had appeared because they had granted Freya's watery wish.

"Well done, girls!" called Oceane, swimming up to the boat.

"The Secret Princesses gave us a message," said Coral. "They said to use your ruby slippers to come back to the palace when you're finished with your boat ride."

The mermaids dived down into the water
and disappeared just as the other kids came
back up on deck.

"Hey, Grandad," said Eden. "What's the
boat called?"

"It hasn't got a name yet," said Grandad.
"As Josh was captain of the winning team,
he can name it."

"No," said Josh, shaking his head. "Freya
can decide what to call the boat. We
wouldn't have won if it wasn't for her."

"How about *Passing Wind?*" called out one
of the boys.

Everyone giggled.

"No," said Freya, shaking her head. "I'm
going to call it *Mermaid Magic*."

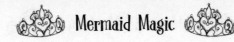

"Ooh!" said Eden. "I really like that, Pipsqueak."

Mia and Charlotte smiled at Freya. They loved the name too!

"Speaking of names," Freya reminded her sister, "what did we agree about calling me Pipsqueak?"

"Oops! Sorry, Freya," said Eden.

"You've proved that size really doesn't matter," said Josh, smiling.

"We should probably head back now," said Grandad. "So the other team can have a turn." He put his sailor's hat on Freya's head. "Do you want to drive?" he asked her.

"Aye, aye, Captain Grandad," she replied with a giggle.

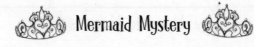

Mia and Charlotte helped Freya hobble
to the prow of the boat. Freya stood at the
wheel, helping her grandfather steer the boat
back towards Hidden Cove.

As they got closer to the bay, Charlotte
could see the other team waiting on the
dock. But so were Princess Poison and Hex!

Josh's team trooped off the boat and down
the dock. But when Mia and Charlotte tried
to get past, the baddies blocked their way.

"I suppose you're off to Wishing Star
Palace now," said Princess Poison. "So why
don't you give my old friends a message from
me? Tell them I'm going to use every last
drop of power to make sure you never break
my curse."

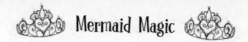

"No. I won't pass on your message," said Charlotte. "Because it's not true."

"We're going to fix the Blue Lagoon," said Mia. "And we'll earn our combs too."

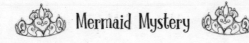

Freya limped up to Princess Poison. "You are not nice at all," she said.

Startled, Princess Poison took a step back – and fell off the dock!

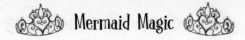

"Help!" she cried, her arms windmilling wildly.

SPLASH! Princess Poison hit the water.

"Mistress!" cried Hex. He reached his hand out to help her up, but when Princess Poison grabbed it she pulled him in too!

"You idiot!" shrieked Princess Poison, thrashing in the water.

"Enjoy your swim!" Charlotte called over her shoulder as she and Mia helped Freya down the dock.

"We've got to go now," Mia told Freya.

"I know," Freya said.

"I hope your ankle feels better," said Mia.

"It's feeling much better already," said Freya, flexing it up and down.

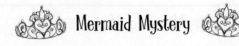

Charlotte looked down at her own feet and saw that her ruby slippers had magically appeared. Mia was wearing hers, too.

They hugged Freya goodbye. Then, holding hands, Mia and Charlotte clicked the heels of their ruby slippers together.

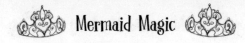

"Wishing Star Palace!" they called.

WHOOSH!

Magic whisked the girls away from the lake to a swimming pool surrounded by palm trees – and princesses! The Secret Princesses were relaxing on sun loungers as the mermaids swam in the turquoise water. Spotting the girls, the princesses clapped their hands and the mermaids slapped their tails against the water appreciatively.

"Great work, girls," said Princess Alice, going over to Mia and Charlotte. She touched her wand gently to Charlotte's necklace and a bluey-green jewel appeared on the pendant. Then Alice added an aquamarine to Mia's necklace.

"It's beautiful," said Mia, admiring the gem. "It's the colour the Blue Lagoon's water used to be."

"And will be again," Charlotte promised.

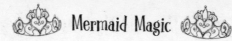

"Will you bring us back to the palace soon so we can break Princess Poison's spell?" asked Mia.

"Of course," said Alice. "But right now you should probably get back home."

"See you soon," Mia said, hugging Charlotte goodbye.

"To grant more watery wishes!" said Charlotte, hugging her best friend back.

As the princesses and mermaids called out

farewells, Alice waved her wand and magic carried the girls away.

In the blink of an eye, Charlotte was back at the crazy golf course. She hurried back to where her family was waiting.

"Hey, Charlotte," called Liam. "Mum and Dad say we can get ice cream."

"Race you to the ice cream stand!" cried

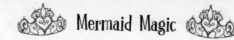

Harvey, running off.

Charlotte sprinted off, then slowed to a jog. She decided to let her little brothers win for a change. After all, she and Mia had just defeated Princess Poison – and that was the very best victory of all!

The End

Join Charlotte and Mia in their next
Secret Princesses adventure,

Sea Turtle Song

read on for a sneak peek!

"I've been dying to come here!" said Mia
Thompson excitedly. A bell tinkled as she
opened the door and stepped inside the
Ceramics Café with a group of her friends
from school.

It was her friend Connie's birthday,
and Connie's mum had taken the girls to
paint pottery at a new place that had just

opened in town. On one side of the bright and sunny café was a wall with shelves of plain white mugs, plates and bowls, as well as adorable ceramic figurines shaped like fairies, unicorns and dinosaurs. On the other wall hung beautifully decorated ceramic plates, the bright colours glazed and shiny.

"OK, girls," said Connie's mum. "Everyone can choose something to paint."

"How are we ever going to pick?" wondered Mia. She loved doing arts and crafts and wished she could paint everything in there!

"I'm going to paint a ballerina," said Connie, who took dance classes.

"Someone help me choose!" wailed

Annabelle. She was holding a bowl in one hand, and a cute puppy figurine in the other.

"This one," said Mia, pointing at the puppy. She loved animals, so puppies got her vote every time!

Yasmina chose a big mug. "What are you going to paint, Mia?" she asked.

"Maybe I should decorate a new water bowl for Flossy," Mia said, thinking of her pet cat. Then suddenly she spotted the perfect thing – a trinket box shaped like a heart. "Actually," she said, taking the box off the shelf. "I'm going to paint this."

As Connie's mum ordered a coffee, the girls put on aprons and sat down at a long table with jars of paint in the middle. At the table next to them, a mum and dad were holding their baby boy. They painted his feet with red paint and gently pressed them on to a plate, stamping it with his tiny footprints.

"Aw," said Annabelle. "That's so cute."

At another table, a group of grown-up ladies chatted as they decorated fruit bowls and vases with colourful patterns.

Dipping their paintbrushes into the pots of paint, Mia and her friends started painting their own items.

Read *Sea Turtle Song* to find out what happens next!

How to Organise a Treasure Hunt

Treasure hunts take a bit of planning but they are always lots of fun. Why not plan one for your friends the next time they come to play?

1. Gather your treasure. It could be chocolate coins, plastic jewellery or little toys and trinkets.

2. Plan your clues. You could give your friends a map, draw pictures, or write riddles for your friends to solve. Here are a few clues to inspire you:

You'll find me on a bed, where you rest your weary head. (Hide the next clue under a pillow.)

I have two hands but no fingers. (Hide the next clue by a clock.)

Normally I am green, but in the autumn I change colour. (Hide the next clue by a tree.)

3. Hide the clues. Make sure your friends aren't around when you do this!

4. Gather your friends around and give them their first clue. Explain what the boundaries are – for example, all the clues are hidden in the back garden or in the house.

5. If your friends are stuck, give them a hint.

6. Celebrate when they find the treasure!

Secret PRINCESSES

What would you wish for?

Are you a Secret Princess?

Join the Secret Princesses Club at:

secretprincessesbooks.co.uk

Explore the magic of the
Secret Princesses and discover:

♥ Special competitions! ♥
♥ Exclusive content! ♥
♥ All the latest princess news! ♥